Buster

The Little Garbage Truck

By Marcia Berneger

Illustrated by Kevin Zimmer

Little Buster could hardly wait until he was big.

"We'll work together," he told Daddy. "We'll be the best garbage trucks in the whole world."

"Be sure you practice, son," said Daddy. "Practice makes perfect."

Buster practiced being fast.

Varoom! Varoom!

"Look out, Kitty!" he called.

Kitty jumped onto his cab. He zipped her around the garage.

Buster practiced being strong. He lifted soup cans and paper cups high over his head. Usually they were empty.

But not always . . . Oops!!

Buster practiced being loud. He honked his horn. Beep!

"A little louder, Buster. People need to hear you," said Daddy. "Try it like this."

HONK!

Buster zoomed close to Mommy. The loud horn frightened him.

"How about coming to work with me, son?" said Daddy.

"I get to go to the truck yard!" Buster was so excited he almost had an accident.

Garbage trucks rumbled all around the truck yard. When a huge front loader revved his engine behind them, Buster nearly jumped out of his tires.

"Attention!" called the front loader. "Let's give Buster our truck-yard welcome."

The garbage trucks circled around.

Buster flashed his headlights. "Hi, everyone," he beeped.

HONK! HONK! HONK! HONK!

Buster skidded to Daddy's side.

Later Buster heard Daddy whispering to Mommy. "He wouldn't leave my side for hours. I didn't know what to do."

A tear slid down Buster's grill. He wanted to be brave, but the trucks in the yard were so big and noisy.

How could he work with Daddy and his friends when their blasting horns and thundering engines scared him?

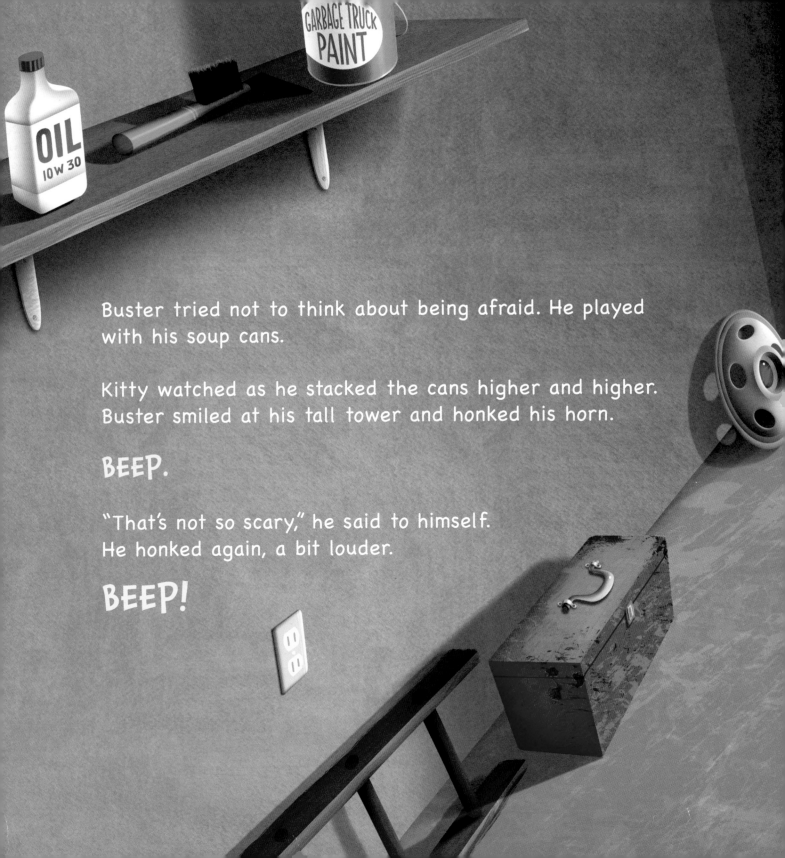

Buster tried not to think about being afraid. He played with his soup cans.

Kitty watched as he stacked the cans higher and higher. Buster smiled at his tall tower and honked his horn.

BEEP.

"That's not so scary," he said to himself.
He honked again, a bit louder.

BEEP!

"I can do this. I'm not afraid!" shouted Buster.
"Daddy, Mommy, come watch me honk my horn!"

HONK!

Buster's tall tower wobbled.

CRASH!

Buster jumped so high he bounced when he landed. "Aw, even my toys scare me," he cried.

"Keep practicing, son. You'll get it," said Daddy as he left for work.

"Why don't you go for a drive, Buster?" said
Mommy. "It will help you feel better."

Buster putt-putted out of the garage
with Kitty beside him.

They rounded the corner and Kitty raced ahead,
checking out the trash in the cans. She swiped
at some yarn in one and snagged an old toy
mouse from another. Kitty disappeared
into the next garbage can.

Daddy was up the street lifting garbage cans and dumping the trash into the huge container on his back. He didn't see Kitty. His long side arm reached out and grabbed the garbage can.

"Jump out, Kitty!" called Buster. But he was too far away. Kitty didn't hear him.

Daddy's engine roared and the garbage can rose high into the air.

"I've got to stop Daddy before it's too late!" Buster raced forward.

"WAIT!" he shouted just as Daddy honked his air horn.

HONK!

Buster froze. His whole frame rattled with fear. He shifted into reverse and backed away from the loud horn.

Meow! cried Kitty.

"Oh, no!" Buster shifted gears and sped forward. He squeezed his eyes shut and blasted his air horn.

"STOP!"

Daddy stopped. He looked in his mirror and saw Kitty.
He lowered the garbage can.

Kitty jumped out. She rubbed up against Buster, purred, and dropped the toy mouse at his wheels.

"That was an awesome honk, son," said Daddy.

Daddy and Buster returned to the truck yard. The garbage trucks all circled around.

"Your kitty would have been a goner if not for you," said the recycle truck.

"Your dad has the loudest air horn around," said the green waste truck. "But he heard your blast over his."

Daddy beamed. "That's my boy!"

"Let's hear that horn, Buster," said the front loader.

Buster squeezed his eyes shut, drew in a deep breath and . . .

HONK!